STAR TREK
FEDERATION

TRAVEL GUIDE

An *Original* Publication of POCKET BOOKS

POCKET BOOKS, a division of Simon & Schuster Inc.
1230 Avenue of the Americas, New York, NY 10020

ISBN: 0-671-00978-8

First Pocket Books trade paperback printing July 1997

10 9 8 7 6 5 4 3 2 1

POCKET and colophon are registered trademarks of Simon & Schuster Inc.

Printed in the U.S.A.

STAR TREK®
FEDERATION

TRAVEL GUIDE

Michael Jan Friedman

POCKET BOOKS
NEW YORK LONDON TORONTO SYDNEY TOKYO SINGAPORE

USING YOUR TRAVEL GUIDE

The purpose of this Travel Guide is to make your voyage through Federation space and beyond as comfortable and enjoyable as possible, regardless of your physical and cultural orientations.

We, the editors, attempt to accomplish this by providing reliable information regarding attractions, lodgings, and restaurants on various planets and facilities ... by pointing you in the direction of what we consider the galaxy's "BEST BETS" ... and by advising you of the dangers and pitfalls a sentient being may encounter along the way.

To use this book effectively, you should be conversant with the Travel Guide's RATING SYSTEM, which employs a variety of symbols. Please familiarize yourself with the chart below and its explanations of those symbols before reading further.

RATING SYSTEM

LOCAL ATTRACTIONS

★★★   worth spanning the galaxy for

★★   fascinating

★   looks better in the holobrochure

RESTAURANTS

🍴🍴🍴   for only the most discriminating palate

🍴🍴   good but not great

🍴   you're better off using a replicator

LODGINGS

💼💼💼   fit for a Grand Nagus

💼💼   clean and comfortable

💼   the brig would be an improvement

Be aware that no attraction, lodging, or restaurant pays for its rating. Each one is evaluated on the basis of merit alone. Evaluations are updated every Federation-standard year.

Please read on.

I know what you're thinking ... no, really, I do. I am, after all, a Betazoid. You're asking yourself if you're prepared to strike out on a great and awe-inspiring tour of the known universe. And the answer is ... of course you're not.

My dear, no one is.

At least not until you've had a chance to peruse this little gem of a guidebook, with its storehouse of information on what to see, do, buy,

eat, and avoid in this exquisite and intriguing galaxy of ours.

As a Federation ambassador of longer standing than I care to admit, I can tell you things aren't always what they appear to be. What you think may be a part of the furniture in some far-off lodging may turn out, in fact, to be your host. Or vice versa. What you intend as a gesture of disgust may be construed as a marriage proposal on one world (or a challenge on another.)

That's why it's always good to study a culture, its customs, and its accommodations before you beam to a planet's surface. The deeper your understanding of the traditions and lifestyles of other species and civilizations, the more pleasant and comfortable your visit will be.

Trust me, you don't want to insult a Ferengi with an insufficient gratuity when he provides you with a service—on Ferenginar, it's a criminal offense. You don't want to engage a Vulcan in a philosophical debate unless you've got several hours to kill. And you never, ever want to get between a Klingon and his bloodwine.

The Federation Travel Guide. I find it helpful. You, my dear, will find it indispensable. I just know you will.

Sincerely,
LWAXANA TROI
Ambassador to the Federation, Daughter of the Fifth House, Holder of the Sacred Chalice of Rixx, and Heir to the Holy Rings of Betazed

BEST BETS

*The best place in
the galaxy to...*

...*play a fierce game of dom-jot.*

STARBASE EARHART

The base's infamous Bonestell Recreational Facility always boasts its share of unsavory types—and then some—so the faint of heart should seek their thrills elsewhere.

But if you're a dom-jot fanatic—and who isn't?—you'll find more and better competition at Bonestell than anywhere in known space.

...*watch a baseball game.*

CESTUS III

There are actually six teams on this colony world dedicated to the ancient Earth pastime. As of this writing, the two best squads were the Cestus Comets and the Pike City Pioneers.

If you catch a contest between these two power-houses, keep an eye out for slick-fielding third baseman "Junior" Yates, who reminds many a visitor of the legendary Buck Bokai.

... enjoy a plate of haggis.

CALDOS COLONY

Founded a century ago, this Federation settlement was patterned after Earth's Scottish Highlands, a region of brooding skies and rolling green hills where sheep's stomach was transformed into a delicacy called **haggis**.

In Caldos colony, the craft of preparing this dish has been raised to an art form. Don't believe it? Try it and see.

... take a mudbath.

THE PARALLAX COLONY ON SHIRALEA VI

The colony is populated by fanciful humanoids who exist purely for the pursuit of pleasure.

And what could be more pleasing than squishing mud between your tactile appendages? Or watching your progeny do the same?

A word of advice: pack a lunch and plan to spend all day in the baths. Once you get in, you won't want to get out.

THE
TOUR

BETAZED

Whether strolling in Betazed's gardens, dining in one of its many fine restaurants, or auditing classes at its renowned university, even the casual visitor will be impressed with the natives' sense of optimism and tranquility.

But then, as telepaths, Betazoids have access to a community of benign and encouraging minds, all of which must be quite a comfort to the individual. Fortunately for the galactic traveler, Betazoids are taught early on to respect the privacy of others—and of visitors in particular.

Be aware, however, that privacy is less of an issue at a Betazoid wedding, where the proceedings are carried out in the nude.

LOCAL ATTRACTIONS

★ ★ ★ **The University of Betazed** is recognized as one of the most advanced institutions of higher learning in the quadrant.

★ ★ **The mansions** of Betazed's exalted houses are ornate and on occasion breathtaking. If you can visit only one, see the Fifth House, which displays the Sacred Chalice of Rixx and the Holy Rings of Betazed.

★ ★ **Janaran Falls** is a spectacular sight and it boasts an impressive array of long-lived muktok plants. Their bristle-like foliage makes a pleasant sound when shaken.

RESTAURANTS

🍴🍴🍴 **The Oskoid**, a vegetarian establishment, is named after a leaflike delicacy native to Betazed. This is where you'll find perhaps the finest food and the most attentive service on the planet.

🍴🍴 **Apolloni's Retreat**, a casual seaside venue, makes up in clever preparations and large portions what it lacks in elegance. If you do nothing else on this world, try the specialty of the house—a dessert called uttaberry pudding.

LODGINGS

🏠🏠🏠 **The Mountain House** at Lake Cataria is an exemplar of hospitality. The sunsets there are beautiful. Swimming is permitted in the warmer months.

KEY PHRASE:
"May good fortune attend you."

UNIT OF CURRENCY:
the Federation credit.

THE AMUSEMENT
PARK PLANET

Located in the Omicron Delta region, this unassuming planet is, in a very real sense, anything you want it to be. The amusement park planet, as it is commonly known, is equipped with sophisticated subterranean equipment capable of reading the minds of its visitors—then almost instantly creating whatever that visitor is thinking about.

Care to ride the elephants on which Earth's Hannibal crossed the Alps. .trade blows with Kahless the Unforgettable . .or explore the hive-caverns of Andoria?

It's all accessible on this world, all yours for the imagining. And it's all absolutely free, thanks to the generosity of the planet's ancient designers. What's more, there's no possibility of injuring yourself in any of your experiences here, despite appearances to the contrary.

The only etiquette you need to observe is a basic consideration for the planet's other visitors. Try not to intrude on their fantasies and they won't be tempted to intrude on yours. Come to think of it, that's a good rule no matter where you go.

LOCAL ATTRACTIONS

★★★ Have anything your heart desires.

RESTAURANTS

🍴🍴🍴 There's no end of possibilities.

LODGINGS

🏨🏨🏨 The sky is the limit.

KEY PHRASE:
"I wish. ."

UNIT OF CURRENCY:
inapplicable.

Trill is a world best known for its "joined" inhabitants, the beneficiaries of an intimate symbiotic union between the planet's two sentient life-forms, the humanoid Trill and a species of small vermiform symbionts. Most of the personality traits and memories of the combined life-form are contributed by the symbionts, who are extremely long-lived.

So while a visitor to Trill may believe he is speaking with a young man, he may actually be conversing with an accumulation of personalities —only some of which may be male and almost none of which are young. In effect, the symbionts are living time capsules, preserving the values and customs of Trill antiquity.

LOCAL ATTRACTIONS

★★★ **The Teneran ice cliffs**, located in the coldest reaches of the Southern Hemisphere, are two hundred feet high and absolutely spectacular. They're at their most colorful just before dusk.

★★ **The caves of Mak'ala** contain interconnecting pools that stretch for kilometers underground. Unfortunately, the most interesting part—the breeding environment for the Trill symbionts—is a restricted area.

★★ **The Baths of Trill** are open and airy, a nice place for a picnic.

RESTAURANTS

🍴🍴 **The Interplanetary Bar and Grill** features Kohlanese stew, Maraltian seev-ale, and white chocolate fondue, as well as several hundred other offworld specialties. Unfortunately, local cuisine failed to tempt our reviewer's palate.

LODGINGS

💼 **The Selipsis**, Trill's largest and oldest beach resort, offers visitors an opportunity to commune with this world's unique purple oceans—but, regrettably, not much else. Nonetheless, book ahead of time, especially in-season, as the Selipsis fills up quickly.

KEY PHRASE:
"Grow old in wisdom."

UNIT OF CURRENCY:
The Federation credit.

ANGEL ONE

The inhabitants of this lush green planet are humanoid, very much in the mold of Earth's human species. However, its most distinguishing characteristic is its rather extreme form of matriarchal government. In short, Angel One is ruled by females, all of whom have the right to vote in elections or hold public office, most notably in the ruling six-member council.

By contrast, the males on this planet can do neither. Male visitors to Angel One are advised to treat indigenous females with a level of respect bordering on reverence, much as the native males do. For example, a male is not to turn his back on a female, but rather to back away when leaving a female's presence.

LOCAL ATTRACTIONS

★★★ **The Great Hall**, a lush and architecturally absorbing venue, is the place where Angel One's six-woman council convenes. Tours of the place are available by appointment only—but never when the council is in session.

RESTAURANTS

🍴🍴🍴 **Gutqyrth** is a traditional feasting hall, where diners sit at long tables and share native dishes in a family style atmosphere. As at most eating establishments on this world, any men present are expected to serve the women accompanying them.

🍴🍴 **Manciitu** is an open-air restaurant where musicians perform from the time the sun goes down until the wee hours. Try the roast gaddig with bannuq sauce—unless you're a male, that is. Only females are welcome here.

LODGINGS

🏨🏨🏨 **Clep'pus Hostel** is located on Angel One's highest mountaintop. The view is to die for. And unlike many other inns on the planet, it accepts reservations from males unescorted by females.

KEY PHRASE: "Yes, Mistress."

UNIT OF CURRENCY: The orad.

EARTH

No planet is so rich in Federation history as the Class-M world called Earth. And no species figures so prominently in Federation history as humankind.

Throughout their early history, humans were driven by the impulse to possess and acquire land. It was this same instinct that propelled mankind into space some four hundred years ago. By the dawning of the twenty-first century, humans had begun to put aside their hunger for territory in favor of a hunger for knowledge.

At the same time, human civilization rose above the bloody

internecine conflicts that had plagued it since its beginnings—conflicts which included three worldwide altercations and the nearly devastating Eugenics Wars in its twentieth century alone.

In 2161, when the United Federation of Planets was founded, Earth became the organization's home base. The Council buildings and Starfleet Academy still stand near San Francisco's Golden Gate Bridge, shining tributes to the Federation's governing principles of cooperation and tolerance.

Tourists are encouraged to stroll through the gardens between Starfleet Command and the Acad-

emy buildings. There are many memorial markers dotting the grounds. The most visited memorial is the one for James T. Kirk, an Academy alumnus.

The Federation Council is also located in San Francisco. Its chambers are open to visitors for several hours a day, even when the council is in session. The only exceptions are those times when Federation security issues are being discussed.

Of course, Earth is more than just the home of the Federation. It's also a multiplicity of cultural viewpoints unrivaled in the known galaxy. Even if you're pressed for time, sample at least a few of these subcultures. You won't regret it.

LOCAL ATTRACTIONS

★ ★ ★ **The Atlantis Project** is an effort to create a small continent in the middle of Earth's Atlantic Ocean—in effect, a terraforming project in miniature. As it's rare for the casual observer to see terraforming in action, a visit here is highly recommended.

★ ★ **Angel Falls** in southeastern Venezuela is the highest waterfall on Earth. A fine spot for a romantic interlude.

★ ★ ★ **Yosemite National Park**, set aside as a nature preserve in 1890, is one of the most beautiful places on Earth. Don't miss El Capitan, a massive monolithic mountain with a sheer granite face almost two kilometers high.

★ ★ **Cambridge University** is an educational institution founded twelve hundred years ago in the British Isles. Much important work has been done there in the areas of mathematics and physics, including Isaac Newton's *Opticks,* Dirac's theories on the existence of positrons, and Stephen Hawking's quantum theory of gravity.

★ ★ **Starfleet Headquarters** and **Starfleet Academy** are open to visitors every day of the year. Cadet-guided tours are also available. The weather is almost always pleasant, though fog may be a factor.

★ ★ **The Federation Council Chambers** are also open to visitors. They are a lot more interesting when the council is in session. Otherwise, there's not much to see.

RESTAURANTS

🍴🍴🍴 **Ping Chow** in Beijing is a Mandarin palace converted into a restaurant. The menu is an imaginative treatment of traditional Chinese dishes. Our favorites were the Beijing duck with ginger marrow and the Emperor's Choice (hacked chicken with a half-dozen unusual dipping sauces).

🍴🍴 At the **Low Note**, also in New Orleans, the food isn't bad. In fact, it's quite good. But it's overshadowed by the quality of the music (jazz) and the ambience (seductive).

🍴 **The Cafe Des Artistes** in Paris, an outdoor establishment, features a view of the ancient Eiffel Tower, as well as such tongue-in-cheek house specialties as

🍴🍴🍴 **Sisko's Creole Kitchen**, in New Orleans, offers a casual atmosphere and some of the best food anywhere … but don't take our word for it. See for yourself.

Croissants D'ilithium, Klingon Targ à la Mode, L'anti-matter Flambé, and Tribbles dans les Blankettes. Would that the chef were as skilled as he is humorous.

🍴🍴 **Chez Sandrine** in Marseilles is a homey place with an excellent wine list. Sandrine, the proprietress, will point you to the best dishes on the menu. Unfortunately, a large portion of the clientele is made up of Starfleet cadets.

LODGINGS

🧳🧳🧳 **The Kremlin,** once the seat of government for the Union of Soviet Socialist Republics, is now the finest hotel on Earth. The "downtrodden" staff likes to joke about how things will be "after the revolution."

🧳 **The House of Ra,** in what was once Egypt, offers an inspiring view of the ancient pyramids, which were burial vaults for Egyptian monarchs. Our advice? See the pyramids— but stay somewhere less pricey.

KEY PHRASE: "Thank you for your assistance."

UNIT OF CURRENCY: The Federation credit.

QO'NOS [KLINGON]

Qo'noS is the homeworld of the Klingons, a proud race of humanoid warriors known throughout the galaxy for their ferocity and their imperial aggression.

When you greet a Klingon warrior, he doesn't say "hello" or "how are you?" He asks: "What do you want?" Perhaps as much as anything else, this illustrates the bluntness—but also the open-handed honesty—that pervades Klingon culture and tradition.

The Federation-Klingon alliance was recently shattered when the Klingons launched a major invasion of Cardassia, which the Federation refused to support. However, recognizing the threat posed by the Dominion to both Klingon and Federation interests, Klingon High Council

leader Gowron later revalidated the alliance.

With diplomatic relations gradually being restored, visitors have begun to return to Qo'nos, drawn by a sense of adventure and a desire to experience Klingon culture firsthand. After all, no civilization in known space boasts a prouder or more colorful tradition.

And nowhere is it more colorful than in Kling, the capital city of Qo'noS, home to the Klingon High Council. Unfortunately, few off-worlders have ever seen the Great Hall where the council meets, and even fewer have survived the experience.

Visitors should ask about the street festivals which re-enact key episodes in the life of Kahless the Unforgettable—the warrior who introduced

Klingons to the concept of honor some fifteen hundred years ago. One of the best known festivals is the Kot'baval, which commemorates the epic battle between Kahless and the Emperor Molor.

Regardless of where you may go in the Empire, one bit of advice always applies: if you challenge a Klingon in any way, shape, or form, you will be called upon to defend yourself—sometimes in a fight to the death.

LOCAL ATTRACTIONS

★ ★ ★ **The Kri'stak Volcano** near Lake Lusor is the site of one of the most stirring Klingon legends. It's here that the mythical Kahless dipped a lock of his hair into the lava flow and created the first bat'leth. If you're lucky, you'll be around when the volcano decides to erupt.

★ ★ **Hem**—literally "to be proud"—is the finest example of Klingon opera house architecture on the planet. Every third night it presents *Aktuh and Melota*, the most beloved Klingon opera of the last hundred years.

★ ★ **Quin'lat**, birthplace of the Klingon poet G'trok, is surrounded by fields full of night-blooming Throgni, the most fragrant of Klingon flowers. It's also notable as the site of a fable in which a foolish man tries to stand up against a powerful wind.

RESTAURANTS

🍴🍴🍴 One of the best dining halls on Qo'noS has no name. It's located off the main square in the ancient village of Tolar'tu. The heart of targ is served bloody and still pumping and the gagh—also known as serpent worms— is very demonstrably alive. Just beware of the clientele, which can be dangerous even from a Klingon point of view.

🍴🍴 **SuQ**, which ironically means "toxic," is one of the most popular eateries in Kling. The food is only adequate, but the bloodwine flows freely and so do the tales of war and vengeance. It's also one of the few places where you can get racht, a larger form of serpent worms.

🍴🍴 **Gre'thor** (the Klingon equivalent of "hell") is genteel by Klingon standards and caters largely to offworld merchants. Located on the outskirts of Kling, it specializes in such dishes as rokeg blood pie, pipius claw, and zilm'kach (a segmented orange foodstuff), which are considered most palatable to non-Klingons.

LODGINGS

🧳 All Klingon hostelries are the same: Spartan at best. In fact, the Klingons pride themselves on the lack of comfort in their sleeping quarters.

KEY PHRASE:
"tajwIj 'oHbe' chorIIj jeqbogh Dochvetlh'e'"

[translation: "That is not my dagger protruding from your midsection."]

UNIT OF CURRENCY:
The darsek, though strips of latinum are also acceptable.

ARGELIUS II

This Class-M planet is one of the most hospitable worlds in the entire Alpha Quadrant. In fact, tourism is its number one industry (shipping running a distant second).

The Argelians are also among the more hedonistic species in the galaxy. Their lives are dedicated to giving and receiving all varieties of pleasure—so much so that they have to hire administrators from other planets.

Lately, the Argelians have begun exporting their hedonistic practices to other worlds and space stations. A good example of this is the spate of Argelian massage facilities that have sprung up lately in some of the most unusual places.

LOCAL ATTRACTIONS

★★★ **The Statue of Pol'is**, the Argelian god of oratory, straddles the harbor at Synthaea. Pol'is is attended by smaller statues of S'ra and Jaa'n, his attendant deities.

★★★ **The Doc'gi** is a five-hundred-year-old garden maintained by disciples of the all-female Order of Juud. As you stroll through, feel free to sample the fruit that grows there—particularly jontin, which is very sweet, and matyu, which is slightly tart.

RESTAURANTS

🍴🍴🍴 **Chuq'ar**, named after its proprietor, is a dining establishment that features native Argelian specialties like braised lyn, roast taad, and buttered ali'i sprouts. Guests are invited to participate in a game of chance called "luu," in which everyone mysteriously breaks even by the time they leave.

🍴🍴🍴 **Michael's Wok** is run by an Earthman who came to Argelius II twenty years ago and fell in love with it. He brings an intriguing Terran style of preparation to traditional dishes like raahn stew, rurii salad, and steamed emmi leaves.

LODGINGS

🏛🏛🏛 **L'yar**, a 100-room hotel with a view of magnificent Katay Lake, offers rooms furnished in the manner of this world's Airic, Cay't and Lyzee dynasties. It also boasts the most venerated massage staff on the planet—so venerated, in fact, that they've set up a teaching center on the grounds.

⛵⛵⛵ **The Miijul**, which means "finally" in the Argelian tongue, is a sailing vessel with capacity for fifty guests. Cruising along the picturesque Do'hna archipelago, you'll be so enchanted by the scenery you'll almost forget to eat. Try to remember, however, because the cooks, Jaec and Ah'lix, make the best smoked fish in the Northern Hemisphere.

KEY PHRASE: "A little to the right, if you please."

UNIT OF CURRENCY: Argelius II has none of its own, but most other forms are accepted.

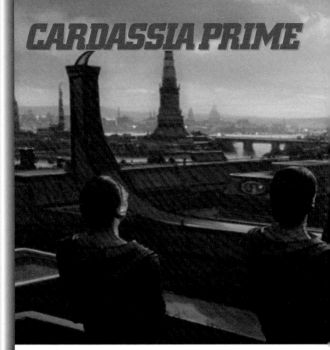

CARDASSIA PRIME

Home to the humanoid Cardassians, Cardassia Prime is a planet poor in natural resources, though in ancient times it boasted a splendid civilization whose ruins are still in evidence.

Unfortunately, this world is not open to tourism. In allying themselves with the Dominion of the Gamma Quadrant, the Cardassians have cut themselves off from their neighbors. On the other hand, Cardassian politics have been rather volatile. We offer the following information in the hope that Cardassia Prime will once again host Federation visitors.

The Cardassians are a study in contrasts—at

times coldhearted to the point of ruthlessness and at other times compassionate to the point of sentimentality. Watching a Cardassian weep at the death of his child's pet wompat, you would have a difficult time imagining him cutting down an enemy without blinking. Yet he will.

The Cardassians have always prided themselves on their intellectual achievements. For instance, all citizens enjoy photographic memories as the result of intense mind-training programs during early childhood.

These people also have a great reverence for their artists—among them

Iloja of Prim, a serialist poet from the days of the First Republic, whose temper forced him into exile on Vulcan for a time. The best example of the Cardassian novel is a multigenerational epic entitled *The Never Ending Sacrifice*, which provides insight into the Cardassian notion of duty to family and state.

The visitor to Cardassia Prime would do well to steer clear of the criminal justice system, which grants no rights at all to the accused. Rather, it serves to reinforce Cardassian cultural norms.

LOCAL ATTRACTIONS

★★★ The well-known novel *Meditations on a Crimson Shadow*, by Preloc, provides a veritable walking tour through the handsome **Loo Wess** region of Cardassia. High points are the fountain of Senndi, the peak of Errqa, the valley of Hrabin, and the caverns of Ani.

★ The **Colaxa Plain** is home to the only real wild gettle left on Cardassia. However, this once-mighty herd has been decimated by poachers, making it less impressive than in days gone by.

★ **Rebron Arena**, outside the capitol, is the site of a weekly series of bloody vole fights—which the Cardassians dearly love to gamble on. The Cardassian vole,

not to be confused with the mild-mannered Terran rodent of the same name, is a vicious creature with an insatiable appetite, razor-sharp teeth, and a highly developed sense of territoriality.

RESTAURANTS

🍴🍴 **The Gul**, an eating establishment within walking distance of the courts, is the only one worth considering. The menu includes a broad selection of Cardassian delicacies, including tojal in yamok sauce, regova eggs, and zabo steak. We recommend you wash it down with kanar or, if you're in a more mellow mood, rokassa juice. For a satisfying ending, try the larish pie.

LODGINGS

🛏 **Legate's Choice** is a small, somber place, but it's the best Cardassia has to offer the offworld visitor. With the exception of government officials, most Cardassians don't travel much; and when they do, they stay with friends.

KEY PHRASE:
"Do you doubt my sincerity?"

UNIT OF CURRENCY:
The lek.

VULCAN

The humanoid inhabitants of this world were once a passionate, violent people whose civilization was ravaged by war. Some two thousand years ago, the philosopher Surak convinced the Vulcans to suppress their turbulent emotions in favor of a doctrine that embraced pure logic. This became known as the Time of Awakening.

Vulcan society is now based entirely on logic; any trappings of emotion are considered socially unacceptable. (Visitors are advised to keep their own emotional displays private for the duration of their stay.)

The only known exception to the Vulcan's devotion to logic is the traditional mating ritual, based on a time when male Vulcans killed to obtain their mates. However, the ceremony is steeped in

secrecy and is not open to outsiders.

Much has been said about the Vulcan mind-meld, not all of it true. Simply put, a mind-meld is a telepathic link initiated by physical contact between two individuals, only one of whom needs to be a Vulcan. It is considered a deeply personal encounter, one unlikely to be shared with casual visitors.

The traveler must always keep in mind that Vulcan is not a friendly environment to many species. Its heat, high gravity, and dry, thin atmosphere place a great physical strain on most offworld sentients who spend any time there.

Also, the Vulcan sun can damage sight organs. Native Vulcans have a secondary eyelid to protect their eyes against naked sunlight, but visitors should consider sun visors.

Vulcans are long-lived. It's not unusual for them to reach two hundred fifty years old without showing any loss of intellectual capacity.

LOCAL ATTRACTIONS

★★★ The capital city of **ShariKahr** is an absolutely enchanting place. The simple but elegant buildings, the delicate and meticulously maintained sand gardens, and the imaginative statuary all work together to bring visitors a sense of peace.

★★★ Vulcan's **wilderness preserves**, of which there are many, give one a sense of how rugged and full of predators the land remains outside the major cities.

★★★ The peak of **Mount Seleya** is the site of an ancient Vulcan temple. Visitors are permitted to see this relic of the planet's violent past only from afar—but even then, it's a magnificent spectacle.

★★ **The Vulcan Science Academy** is an institution of higher learning known and respected throughout the galaxy. Unfortunately, lectures tend to be dry by the standards of most sentient species.

RESTAURANTS

🍴 **Piar'ash**, which translates as "excellence," is a world-renowned dining hall in the city of Vulcana Regar which caters almost exclusively to native Vulcans. That is because most other species find Vulcan food bland—and this place is no exception. Beware of the Vulcan port, a green after-dinner drink which can be highly intoxicating to non-Vulcans.

🍴🍴 **Insight** is an eatery which has taken traditional Vulcan dishes and spiced them up for the off-world palate. The steamed Vulcan mollusks are fine by themselves but even better when served in Rhombolian butter. And nowhere will you sample a tastier plomeek soup.

LODGINGS

🧳🧳🧳🧳 **The Sehlat,** named for a Vulcan animal resembling a Terran "teddy bear" with six-inch fangs, is one of the few luxury inns in ShariKahr. Reserve a room designed especially with your species in mind.

🧳🧳 **The Meditation** is a thoroughly Vulcan establishment, simple and sparsely furnished. However, all of its sixty-seven rooms offer a view of the stately statue of Surak in Serenity Square.

KEY PHRASE:
"Live long and prosper."

UNIT OF CURRENCY:
The Federation credit.

FERENGINAR

The Ferengi are a techno-
logically advanced
humanoid civilization
first encountered by the
Federation in 2364. Fer-
engi society is highly reg-
ulated and ruthlessly
embraces the principles
of capitalism. On Ferenginar, everything is nego-
tiable and anything can
be had for the right
amount of latinum.

Tipping isn't just rec-
ommended—it's manda-
tory. Conveniences that
are taken for granted in
other civilizations come
loaded with fees and levies
among the Ferengi. As the
weather is almost always
rainy, save yourself some

money and bring your own umbrella.

The Ferengi welcoming ceremony offers insight into the Ferengi value system. In this ceremony, the host says: "Welcome to our home. Place your imprint on the legal waivers and deposit your admission fee in the box by the door. Remember, my house is my house." The guest replies: "As are its contents."

The visitor will often hear references to "lobes." Taken literally, they refer to a Ferengi's ears. Figuratively, they refer to his prowess as a businessman.

The Ferengi Rules of Acquisition are not laws, but guidelines for proper behavior. Children are expected to memorize them—all 285—and repeat them on command. The first rule is, "Once you have their money, you never give it back." Several other rules indicate that family and friends are less important than paying customers—unless, of course, you can exploit family and friends for profit.

Only Ferengi males are seen in public. If you are invited to a Ferengi home, be aware that females are not allowed to wear clothing. It's also illegal for females to earn profit, talk to strangers, or recite the Rules of Acquisition. And at mealtime, they're expected to chew the food of all males at the table.

LOCAL ATTRACTIONS

★★★ **The Sacred Marketplace**, which thrives in the long shadow of the Tower of Commerce, is the only true attraction on Ferenginar. However, it is well worth the trip. Nowhere else is the Ferengi spirit of free trade so evident as in this ancient plaza, where stall keepers haggle over the last little detail of even the most insignificant transaction.

★ **Arg's Tongo Parlor and Holosuite Emporium** is the best-known establishment of its kind. However, it's no more exciting or less expensive than any of the other tongo parlors on Ferenginar—and there are tens of thousands of them. (Tongo is a popular game of chance on Ferenginar.)

RESTAURANTS

🍴🍴🍴 **The 214th Rule**, Ferenginar's most elegant dining establishment, is named after the Ferengi rule of acquisition that states, "Never begin a business transaction on an empty stomach."

The food is as good as the ambiance. Try the flaked blood fleas and the baked locar beans for starters. Then dig into a plate of tube grubs—a delicacy best served alive and slimy—and wash it down with some Gamzain wine.

🍴🍴 **Gulda's All-You-Can-Eat Day-or-Night Fine Dining House** offers its clientele anything they want—for a price. Of course, the more exotic the request, the more expensive one's meal is likely to be.

LODGINGS

🛏🛏🛏 **The Nagus** offers such brazenly lavish accomodations, many sentient beings will find it shameful. Owned by Grand Nagus Zek, this veritable pleasure palace has no equal in terms of the splendor of its furnishings, the richness of

its cuisine, or the lengths to which its staff will go to satisfy your every desire.

▮▮▮▮▮ Frin's Taverns—of which there were 31 locations at last count—offer comfortable, quiet accomodations with friendly, helpful staffs. Certainly not the best on Ferenginar, but also not the worst.

▮▮ Rekka's Place—Ferenginar's largest hotel chain with nearly two thousand locations—gives you a bed, a light, and a heatsource, but not much more. It's basic, basic, basic. But then, as the hosts of these places will surely remind you, you get what you pay for.

KEY PHRASE:
"I just saw that somewhere else for half the price!"

UNIT OF CURRENCY:
Gold-pressed latinum, in slips, strips, or bars. Any currency is welcome.

GARAK'S TAILOR SHOP

TELL US EVERYTHING

At **GARAK'S TAILOR SHOP**, we don't just fashion clothing. We fashion images, personalities, dreams of oneself that transcend function and even style.

But to accomplish this, to make you a living, breathing masterpiece, you must share something of yourself. Your hopes, your fears, your secret desires—not to mention those of your friends and co-workers.

In return, we will share the tailoring skills that have earned us accolades in the farthest corners of the galaxy.

And don't worry—we won't breathe a word of what you confide in us. At **GARAK**'s, we always play it . . . close to the vest.

The population of this world is humanoid, though at any given time it's vastly outnumbered by the hordes of offworld tourists who flock to its endless string of climate-controlled jungle islands.

There's a good reason for this torrent of visitors. No other planet in known space is so completely devoted to sensuality. To facilitate a sexual liaison—known as *jamaharon*—it is customary to carry a special statuette called a Horga'hn.

However, sex is only one of the many pleasing activities offered on Risa. Guests may also skinny-dip in one of the galaxy's most picturesque hot springs, take a relaxing reyamilk soak, or simply bask in the soothing light of Risa's dual suns.

LOCAL ATTRACTIONS

★ ★ ★ Risa itself is the attraction—all of it, from its glittering, sun-drenched beaches to . . . well . . . its other glittering, sun-drenched beaches.

RESTAURANTS

🍽️🍽️🍽️ While there aren't any restaurants per se, any kind of cuisine can be obtained anywhere on Risa, at any time. What's more, it's all of the highest quality.

LODGINGS

🧳🧳🧳 Every guest suite on this world offers a stunning view of some-thing—usually the gentle surf washing up along the sensuous coastline. The service and the accomoda-tions are simply the best in the known galaxy.

KEY PHRASE:
"Why didn't I try this before?"

UNIT OF CURRENCY:
Though Risa has no currency of its own, every valid form is accepted here.

BAJOR

Situated in the Denorios Belt, which borders on Cardassian space, the Class-M world known as Bajor was long known for its abundant natural resources and the spirituality of its populace.

Bajorans remain deeply spiritual. However, the decades-long occupation of the planet by Car-dassia destroyed many ancient temples and works of art, and the planet itself has been stripped of its most valu-able resources.

Visitors are advised to learn something about Bajoran religion, as it per-vades so much of the Bajo-rans' daily life. The principal figures in the

Bajoran faith are the Prophets—divine beings credited with being the source of wisdom and enlightenment.

The Prophets are said to dwell in the Celestial Temple, which is located in the Bajoran wormhole. Thus, any commerce the Bajorans may have with the wormhole is a reli-gious experience as well as a secular one.

The most important holiday on Bajor is its Gratitude Festival. Participants write down their problems on Renewal Scrolls and then place them in a special brazier for burning. In this way, one may symbolically reduce one's troubles to

ashes. "Peldor joi" is the greeting traditionally employed during the festival.

Bajorans also have other ways of celebrating their faith. For instance, most Bajorans wear an ornamental earring on their right ear, a symbol of their spiritual devotion. And at mealtime, a chime is rung to give thanks for the food on the table.

Visitors would do well to remember that, unlike in most cultures, a Bajoran's family name comes first and their given name comes afterward. Bajorans are not fond of correcting strangers who call them by their last names instead of their first.

LOCAL ATTRACTIONS

★ ★ ★ **The Bajoran wormhole**, visible from the Deep Space Nine space station, is a three-hour journey from Bajor. Our researcher said he would have traveled a thousand times that distance to behold a sight so wondrous and moving— and he's not even a Bajoran.

★ ★ **The Fire Caverns**, not far from the city of Shar Rapha, are marvels of nature. No visit to Bajor would be complete without a look at them.

★ ★ **Teirysas Beach** affords an excellent view of the planet's emerald-green oceans. At night, it's also a good place to watch Bajor's several moons climb into the sky. (Technically, one of them is actually a planetoid named Jeraddo.)

RESTAURANTS

🍴🍴🍴 **The Fifth Moon** is nothing to look at, with its simple furnishings and its bare walls, but the food here is Bajoran sea-coast cuisine at its absolute best. We recommend the foraiga, with tuwaly pie for dessert.

🍴🍴 **The Celestial Feast** occupies the shell of an old brewery on the Borris River. As one might expect, it serves the best synthale on Bajor. The food tends to be spicy, since the chef learned his trade in the Janitza Mountains, but it's worth sacrificing a few taste buds to sample his hasperat.

🍴🍴 **Provinces** is an eatery that offers dishes from all over Bajor. It's also one of the few places you can get Pyrellian ginger tea, which was extremely scarce during the Cardassian occupation.

LODGINGS

The Philosopher's House is an inn overlooking the Lorus River. Like many Bajoran guesthouses, its appeal is in its tranquil location rather than in any luxury offered by the rooms themselves.

The Ruins is a rambling and uncommonly appealing inn built around the remains of a two-hundred-thousand-year-old Bajoran temple. Unfortunately, precious little is left of the temple besides rubble and the inn—still under construction—tends to be less than peaceful during work hours.

KEY PHRASE:
"May the Prophets smile on you."

UNIT OF CURRENCY:
The lita.

MAKE YOURSELF AT HOME

Of course, no home <u>we</u> know of boasts the thrill of the sector's most generous dabo tables... the most enchanting array of holofantasy programs this side of Delta Four... and a bartender who genuinely cares.

But then, if you really liked it at home, what would you be doing out here in the first place?

QUARK'S. It's more than a place to drop a few credits while you're waiting for your cargo to be inspected. It's a tradition.

THE MYSTERY OF
Chez Sandrine

EVEN OUR NAME EVOKES THE SPIRIT OF ROMANCE AND ADVENTURE FOR WHICH MARSEILLES'S BISTROS ARE KNOWN THE GALAXY OVER.

TRY YOUR SKILL ON OUR POOL TABLE, WHICH HAS BEEN IN THE FAMILY SINCE BEFORE THE TIME OF NAPOLEON. SAMPLE THE FINE, FRAGRANT WINES WE SELECT DAILY FROM OUR OWN PRIVATE CELLAR. EXCHANGE CLANDESTINE GLANCES WITH ROGUES AND STARFLEET CADETS—AND SOMETIMES BOTH THOSE THINGS ROLLED INTO ONE.

TRULY, CHEZ SANDRINE IS WRAPPED IN MYSTERY. BUT TO US, THE GREATEST MYSTERY IS WHAT TOOK YOU SO LONG TO GET HERE.

PLACES
AND
LIFE-FORMS
TO
AVOID

THE ROMULAN STAR EMPIRE

Although the Romulan homeworlds are reputed to be among the loveliest in the galaxy, Federation citizens are strictly prohibited from crossing the Romulan Neutral Zone to visit them. In fact, any penetration of the zone by either side may be construed as an act of war.

If you find yourself confronted by Romulans, either in space or elsewhere, keep in mind that they are an honorable people. If they are not offended, they are not likely to offend. On the other hand, when they feel the situation calls for it, they are capable of arrogance and cold-blooded violence.

The Romulans are reputed to be an offshoot of the Vulcan race—descendants of those who rejected the pacifist teachings of the Vulcan Surak some two thousand years ago and struck out into space to seek a new home.

Eventually, they established their settlements on Romulus and Remus, now considered their homeworlds.

Those who wish to see something of Romulan culture without violating the Neutral Zone can visit the ruins of the ancient Debrune colonies on Barradas III, Calder II, Dessica II, Draken IV, and Yadalla Prime. The Debrune are believed to be a offshoot of Romulan society.

THE BORG

An immensely powerful civilization that's said to have originated in the Delta Quadrant of the galaxy, the Borg are linked to one another by a group mind— whose mission is to incorporate other species into their collective.

This translates into unremittingly aggressive behavior. No one in the Federation can forget the Borg attack of 2366, in which a single Borg vessel destroyed no less than thirty-nine starships in a failed attempt to reach Earth.

If you sight a cube-shaped vessel—the kind the Borg have been seen in—withdraw as quickly as possible and notify Starfleet authorities. If you're captured by the Borg, you'll be surgically outfitted with cybernetic devices and assimilated into their collective.

VAGRA II

A world in the Zed Lapis sector, its inhabitants are believed to have evolved into a higher plane of existence. In the process, they rid themselves of all that was evil within them. The evil was placed in a life-form called Armus, which still resides on the planet surface. We are advised that Armus is both malevolent and dangerous and has claimed the life of at least one Starfleet officer. Clearly Vagra II is to be avoided at all costs.

MINOS

A lush, forested planet, Minos was once the home of a thriving, technologically advanced civilization. The people of Minos were arms merchants who reached the peak of their prosperity during the Erselrope Wars, but they were all killed when their weapons systems backfired on them. The planet is now uninhabited. However, at least a few Minosian weapons systems seem to have survived and were responsible for the destruction of the *U.S.S. Drake* in 2364. Obviously, you don't want to go there.

THE THOLIANS

A species known for its highly territorial nature, the Tholians have had several hostile run-ins with the Federation over the years. Though diplomatic relations currently exist between the Tholian Assembly and the Federation, we advise caution in dealing with any Tholian vessel you may encounter. One never knows when one may be traveling through a sector they consider theirs.

THE BADLANDS

A region of space near the Cardassian border, the so-called Badlands are rife with dangerous plasma storms. As a result, the area is considered extremely dangerous for space travel. Several ships have been lost there, most recently the *U.S.S. Voyager*.

RURA PENTHE

A frozen, almost uninhabitable planetoid deep

inside of Klingon territory, it's the site of a Klingon prison camp. Rura Penthe is known throughout the galaxy as the "aliens' graveyard," because prisoners there are used as forced labor in the planetoid's dilithium mines. The place is so inhospitable, the prison camp needs no guard towers or electronic frontiers to keep the prisoners from escaping. Even now that diplomatic relations with the Klingons have been restored, give Rura Penthe a wide berth.

THE TERIKOF BELT

This is a region within the badlands, beyond the Moriya system. It contains a number of Class-M planetoids where the Maquis take refuge from Starfleet pursuit. Starfleet Command considers the Maquis to be a terrorist group and advises travelers to avoid this region.

RUBICUN III

This class M planet in the Rubicun star system is home to the seemingly idyllic Edo civilization. However, the penalty for breaking any and all Edo laws is death, no matter how trivial the offense may seem. Though the Edo themselves have no way of enforcing their penalties, a mysterious entity there does—so steer clear.

THE BLACK CLUSTER

This is an astronomical phenomenon believed to have formed some nine billion years ago when hundreds of proto-stars collapsed in close proximity to each other. The resulting formation is fraught with violent, unpredictable gravitational wavefronts. These wavefronts, which can absorb energy, are extremely dangerous to spacecraft operating systems. The Federation science vessel *U.S.S. Vico* was destroyed in the Black Cluster in 2368.

THE GAMMA QUADRANT

Accessible through the Bajoran wormhole, the Gamma Quadrant is home

to a powerful alliance of planetary groups called the Dominion. Through the Jem'Hadar, a warrior species genetically engineered for aggression and brutality, the Dominion has made it clear they do not welcome "incursions" by beings from the Alpha Quadrant. Any travel there should be undertaken with this fact in mind.

TALOS IV

For the last hundred years or so, contact with Talos IV has been a violation of Starfleet General Order 7 and therefore punishable by death. While this penalty may seem extreme, this world is obviously a very dangerous place—not only to the prospective visitor, but to the Federation in general.

SISKO'S
CREOLE KITCHEN

It May Not Be The Fanciest Place on Earth

But if you ever had a taste for down-home Louisiana cooking
and some of the friendliest faces in the Alpha Quadrant,
Sisko's Creole Kitchen is the place you want to be.

Fall in love with the creole shrimp in mandalay sauce.
Sigh over our award-winning bread pudding souffle.
Or sample the pasta boudin,
Nathan's favorite (and he's the cook, so he ought to know).

SISKO'S CREOLE KITCHEN.
When you're not looking for fancy . . . just good.